Saying Thank You Makes Me Happy

By WANDA HAYES
Pictures by FRANCES HOOK

ISBN: 0-87239-353-4

STANDARD PUBLISHING

 Cincinnati, Ohio   3623

God Gave Me

Mother and Daddy

Thank you, Mother, for washing my face.
Umm! The soap smells good.
Thank you for putting my Sunday clothes on me.
I'll stand still for you.
Thank you for combing my hair.
Now I'm ready for breakfast.

Thank you, Daddy, for my nice, warm coat.
Thank you for wrapping my scarf around my
    neck.
Thank you for snapping my cap under my chin,
    where it tickles.
Thank you for putting my mittens on my hands.
Now they won't get cold.

Thank you, God, for the church and for my
    teacher.
Thank you 'cause Mother and Daddy take me to
    church.
Thank you for Mother and Daddy.

God Gives Me Food

Heavenly Father,
  Thank you for food
That my mother fixes
  (It tastes very good);
A tall glass of milk,
  Cold and white,
My bowl full of cereal
  (I eat every bite),
Meat and vegetables,
  Soft mashed potatoes,
Butter and bread,
  Sweet, red tomatoes,
And cake and ice cream
  (A very nice treat);
Thank you for everything
  I like to eat.

         Amen.

God Gives Me Berries

Good, red strawberries!
Daddy and I picked them.
Daddy showed me the ones that were ripe,
    and I pulled them and put them in a basket.

Mommy washed the strawberries.
I like to hold them by the stem and bite the red
    part.
Berries are sweet, and juice runs down my chin.
Sometimes it gets on my hands.

I throw the green parts of the berries away, but I
    eat all the red parts.
Then I wash my hands.
My mouth still tastes like berries, and my tongue
    is very red.
Thank you, God, for berries.

God Gives Me Clothes

My daddy gave me a new coat for my birthday.
I'm a year older now.
My coat is brown and soft like my teddy bear.

"Now put this arm in," Daddy said.
"Now this one."
The coat felt funny. It was crooked.
Daddy fixed it. He buttoned each button—one,
   two, three, four, five buttons.

Then Daddy and I looked in the big mirror.
I liked my new coat.
I laughed, and Daddy laughed, too.
Then he gave me a big hug around the middle.

"Thank you, Daddy, for my coat."

God Gave Me My Dog

I have a little puppy named Sandy. I show Sandy I love him by patting his head and rubbing his neck. His hair feels soft and smooth. Sandy likes for me to pat him.

I take good care of Sandy. I give him good dog food and plenty of water. I play with him and fix his bed for him.

When someone does something for me, I say, "Thank you."

When I take care of Sandy, he licks my face and wags his tail. Licking my face and wagging his tail is how Sandy says "thank you."

Thank you, God, for my dog Sandy.

God Gives Me Birds

One day my mother said, "Come and look out the window, but be very quiet." So I walked on my tiptoes over to the window with Mother. She put a finger over her mouth. "Shhh," she said, as she pointed outside to the tree in our back yard.

There on a big, black branch was a little round dish made out of dry grass. Mother whispered, "That's a bird's nest. Look at the mother bird feeding her babies."

The little birds must have been very hungry because they opened their mouths very wide and made a lot of noise. "Chirp! Chirp! Chirp!" The mother bird gave each baby bird a worm to eat.

Mother said, "God makes sure that every bird has food to eat."

God gives me food, too.

. Thank You, God, for taking care of the birds and for taking care of me.

God Gives Me Flowers

One day Mommy and I planted little brown things called bulbs. Mommy said, "After a while we shall have pretty flowers in our yard."

Every day I looked out at the ground. Every day all I saw was dark, brown dirt.

"When will we have pretty flowers in our yard, Mommy?"

"In a few more days," she said. "Flowers need plenty of water and sunshine before they are ready to grow."

One day I saw something green sticking up out of the ground. "Is that a flower?" I asked Mommy.

"No, it is a leaf. Soon we shall have flowers."

Every day I looked. Every day the leaf was taller. Every day Mommy said, "Our flowers will grow."

After breakfast one day, Mommy said, "Look in the yard today. Look where we planted the bulbs."

I did look. Do you know what I saw? Flowers! God had caused the bulbs to grow into pretty yellow flowers.

God Gives Me Rain

The rain makes a funny sound on my umbrella. Each drop goes "plop," then it rolls down my silky umbrella, "zip." From underneath it looks like a lot of tiny rivers running down the top of my umbrella.

Raindrops run right off my raincoat. Sometimes little drops of water stay on the backs of my hands. They are hard to shake off.

My boots go "splash" when I walk in a little puddle. If I splash too hard, water gets inside my boots. Wet socks don't feel good. Mommy doesn't like them either.

Sometimes I move the toe of one boot back and forth slowly in the water. "Swish. Swish."

Rain is pretty. It's red on my umbrella, green on the grass, and gray on the sidewalk. It's all different colors in the puddles. After it stops raining, little drops of water on grass and leaves shine like diamonds.

Rain makes everything outside smell good.

Thank you, God, for the rain.

God Gives Me
Sunday School

I like to go to Sunday school. My teacher smiles and says, "Come in." I put my money in the basket. That is how we say, "I love you, God."

I like to go to Sunday school. Every Sunday I get to see Paula and Billy and Freddie and Roger. But sometimes one of us is sick.

Sometimes we look at pictures on the table. The one I like best is a picture of Jesus.

We sing and pray and listen. Our teacher tells us a story from God's Book. Teacher asks, "Aren't you glad God gave us Jesus?"

"Yes," we say. Then we close our eyes and pray, "Thank you, God, for Jesus."

I say in my head, where no one else can hear, "Thank you, God, for my teacher and for Sunday school. Amen."

God Gives Me Day

Thank you, God, for mornings
  when I can wake up and wash my face
  and put clean clothes on, all by myself.

Thank you for mornings
  when Mommy gives me a big hug and kiss and
    says,
  "Good morning, dear. What would you like for
    breakfast?"
Thank you for the fun I have playing with my
    doll,
  and with my friends outside in the daytime.

Thank you for the pretty blue sky,
  and the yellow sunshine,
  and the flowers that smell so good,
  and for the bees that hum, "Bzzzz, Bzzzz."

Thank you for afternoons when Daddy comes
    home.
Thank you, God,
  for everything that makes me happy all day
    long.

God Gives Me Night

When I look out the window at night,
   the sky is dark blue and the sun is all gone.
That's so we can sleep.

I see a big, white, shiny moon
   that looks like a big, smiling face.
Sometimes the moonlight shines right in the
   window.
I can see it on the floor,
   and when I put my hand down to touch it,
   the moonlight shines on me.

Everywhere I look in the sky
   there are little white stars that sparkle.

Sometimes I put my eyes next to the window
   and look just as far as I can into the sky.
God is up there where no one can see Him,
   but where He can see everyone.
And He's taking care of people way down here.

God Gives Me Bed

When night comes and it's dark outside, I start to yawn and I'm sleepy. Mommy helps me get ready for bed.

I take a bath and splash a little and have fun. Mommy dries me with a big towel. I climb into my soft, warm pajamas.

After I run and kiss Daddy good night, I get down on my knees beside my bed and talk to God. I say "thank you" to God for Mommy and Daddy, and all the good times I've had that day.